Keiko Kasza

Don't Laugh, Joe!

For Yoshiyuki, Chiaki and Ami

Copyright © Keiko Kasza 1997

All rights reserved.

First published in 1997
by G P Putnam's Sons
a division of The Putnam & Grosset Group
200 Madison Avenue
New York
NY 10016
USA

First published in Great Britain in 1998
by Macdonald Young Books
an imprint of Wayland Publishers Ltd
61 Western Road
Hove
East Sussex
BN3 1JD

A catalogue record for this book
is available from the British Library.

ISBN 0 7500 2522 0

Mother Possum dearly loved her little son Joe, but he was always giggling. Lately his giggling made her worry. Mother Possum was about to teach Joe the most important lesson a possum can learn.

"Joe," said Mother Possum, "you must learn how to play dead."
"Why?" asked Joe.
"Because we possums escape our enemies by playing dead," Mother Possum explained.
"When you learn this trick, Joe, I'll bake you the possums' favourite dessert – a bug pie!"

They started to practise.

"No giggling, Joe," Mother Possum warned.

"No problem, Mum," Joe answered.

Joe played dead, and his mother sniffed his fur
like a hungry fox.

Sniff, sniff, sniff.

Joe laughed so hard that his stomach hurt.

"Can I have my pie now?" he asked.

"No way, Joe," Mother Possum scolded.

"Dead possums don't laugh!"

Joe practised playing dead again. This time his mother poked him like a nasty wolf.
Poke, poke, poke.
Joe laughed so hard that he screamed for her to stop. "Can I have my pie now?" he asked.
"No way, Joe," Mother Possum scolded.
"Dead possums don't scream!"

Joe practised playing dead once more. This
time his mother shook him like a scary tiger.
Shake, shake, shake.
Joe laughed so hard that he wriggled loose
and fell on the floor.
"How about some bug pie, Mum?" he asked.
"No way, Joe," Mother Possum scolded.
"Dead possums don't wriggle!"

Joe's mother was worried about his laughing, but his friends loved it. They liked to watch Joe play dead because he made them laugh, too. "But, Joe," Mother Possum said, sighing, "what will you do when real danger comes?"

One day, Mother Possum took
Joe outside to practise.
"This time," she said. "I'll be a
grumpy old bear. When I growl
at you, you play dead. OK, Joe?"
"Nothing to it, Mum," Joe said.
But just as Mother Possum was
about to growl...

…a real grumpy old bear came out of the woods. He let out the fiercest growl Joe had ever heard. Joe and his mother immediately fell to the ground to play dead.

The grumpy old bear sniffed Joe's fur.
Sniff, sniff, sniff.

The grumpy old bear poked Joe's tummy.
Poke, poke, poke.

Finally, the grumpy old bear shook Joe up and down.
Shake, shake, shake.

Joe didn't laugh. Joe didn't scream. Joe didn't wriggle.
For the first time, he played dead perfectly. Mother
Possum was very proud of him. But the grumpy old
bear wouldn't go away. He sat and sat and sat.

Suddenly, the bear started to cry big tears.
"This is terrible," he moaned. "I'm always so
grumpy. I thought that if anyone could make
me laugh, it would be little Joe the possum.
But when I find him, poor Joe drops dead
before my eyes! Oh, this is awful!"

When he heard the bear's story, Joe was
relieved. He even began to feel sorry for the
sobbing bear. "Hey, Mr Bear," he called,
"I'm not dead, I was just playing dead."

The bear was so surprised he almost jumped
out of his fur. "Playing dead?" he cried.
"Boy, you're good at that! Oh, Joe,"
he cried, "I want to laugh like you!"

"It's easy," said Joe. "Lots of things are funny, Mr Bear. What happened just now is funny." And he started to giggle. Soon his laughter spread to everyone around him, even to the grumpy old bear.

Before long, the animals were laughing
so hard that the whole forest shook.
"Oh, Joe," the bear howled, "thank you
for teaching me to laugh."
"Thank you, Mr Bear," Joe answered,
"for teaching me how to play dead."

"Now can I have my pie?" Joe asked his mother.
"Absolutely," Mother Possum answered.
"Everyone, please come and join us for some
delicious bug pie."
"With grasshoppers!" Joe shouted gleefully.
"And beetles and yummy cockroaches, too!"

The other animals suddenly stopped their giggling.
"Bug pie??? Cockroaches!!!"
One by one, they fell to the ground...

...and played dead.